# MOON LAKE

# M   ON
# LAKE

Story and pictures by Ivan Gantschev
Translated by Marianne Martens

A Michael Neugebauer Book
North-South Books / New York / London

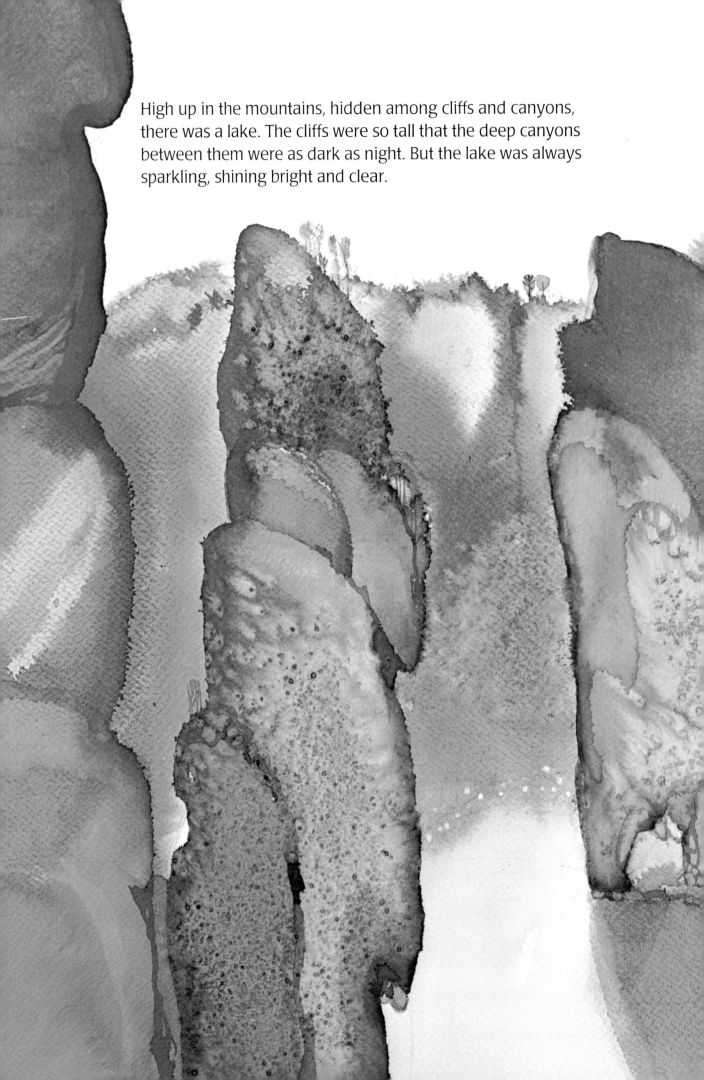

High up in the mountains, hidden among cliffs and canyons, there was a lake. The cliffs were so tall that the deep canyons between them were as dark as night. But the lake was always sparkling, shining bright and clear.

Local people called it Moon Lake. Legend had it that sometimes the moon herself came down to bathe in the ice-cold waters. Afterward, she shook herself dry, showering precious silver stones along the shore. Many had searched for the legendary lake, but always in vain. And some of those who went searching disappeared, lost forever in the rocky wilderness.

There was only one person who knew how to find the lake, an old shepherd who lived high up in the mountains. His small cottage was a day and a night's journey from the nearest town, through thick forests and over steep hills. No one ever made the difficult journey, so the shepherd and his grandson Peter lived a simple life tending the sheep.

One winter, when the paths were completely blocked by snow, the old shepherd could no longer tend to the sheep. He stayed by the fire, and Peter took care of him and the sheep too.

On the coldest day that winter, the shepherd's life began to fade away. As Peter went out to search for firewood, the shepherd watched the dying embers of the fire and remembered the glittering stones along the shore of Moon Lake. He had always meant to show his grandson how to find the lake, but when the fire went out the shepherd died, and the secret of Moon Lake was lost.

Peter stayed on in the cottage by himself,
but he was content. The sheep produced
plenty of milk, which he used to make
cheese that he sold in the town. He made
jam from wild apples, pears, and berries.
He grew his own onions, garlic, and lettuce,
and found nettles, mushrooms, and herbs
all around, and from these he made
delicious warm soups.

One evening, as he was driving the sheep
into their stalls, he noticed that one was
missing.

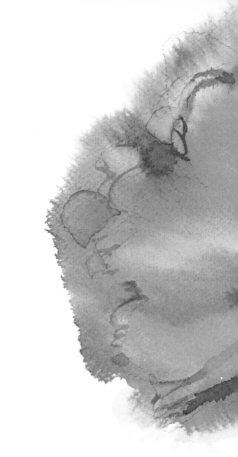

Peter packed some bread and a piece of cheese, and set off to look for the missing sheep. It was already dusk when he reached a deep canyon. From far below came a helpless bleating. Peering over the edge of the cliff, Peter saw a sparkling lake and, on the banks, his poor lost sheep.

Peter found a path between the cliffs, and climbed down. As he descended, the moon rose and began to flood the canyon with a light as bright as day!

When he reached the bottom of the cliff, Peter gasped in amazement.
The banks of the lake were covered with silver stones that glistened
in the moonlight.

"How beautiful!" Peter whispered, and he collected a few stones and
put them in his bag. "If I can sell these stones in the town, I could buy
a new blanket and a shirt. Perhaps I could even buy little bells for
the sheep so that I can find them more easily," he said.

"You could indeed," a voice replied. "But only if you can find
your way out of here."

Peter spun around. Before him stood a large, handsome
silver fox. "I am so hungry," said the fox. "Do you have
anything to eat?"

"I'll give you whatever I have," the boy said. "There's not
much—a little bread and some cheese."

The fox eagerly gobbled up all the food.

Then he turned to Peter. "In return for your kindness,
I will tell you the secret of Moon Lake. You must leave
the lake before dawn, for once the sun rises you will
be blinded by the dazzling stones and you will never
find your way home. Come, I will show you the path."

Peter heaved the sheep onto his shoulders. With the fox's help, he was soon out of the canyon, and there he said good-bye to his new friend. By sunrise he and the sheep were safely back at the little cottage.

Soon after that, Peter made the long journey to town. In the market, he spread out the stones on a cloth and offered them for sale. But before he had sold even one, the king's soldiers arrived, and ordered Peter to go with them to the castle.

The king asked where Peter had found the shimmering stones. Peter told them his story. At that, the king's men seized the stones, and the king demanded to know how to find the secret lake. It was hard for Peter to explain, and when he began to stutter nervously, the king threatened to throw him into a deep well full of snakes if he did not immediately tell him how to get to the lake.

Peter had no choice, so he agreed to escort
the king and his men to Moon Lake. They
rode all night and all the next day, and
when night came again they arrived at the
canyon. As everyone climbed down the
cliffs, the moon rose and shone its beautiful
light on the lake.

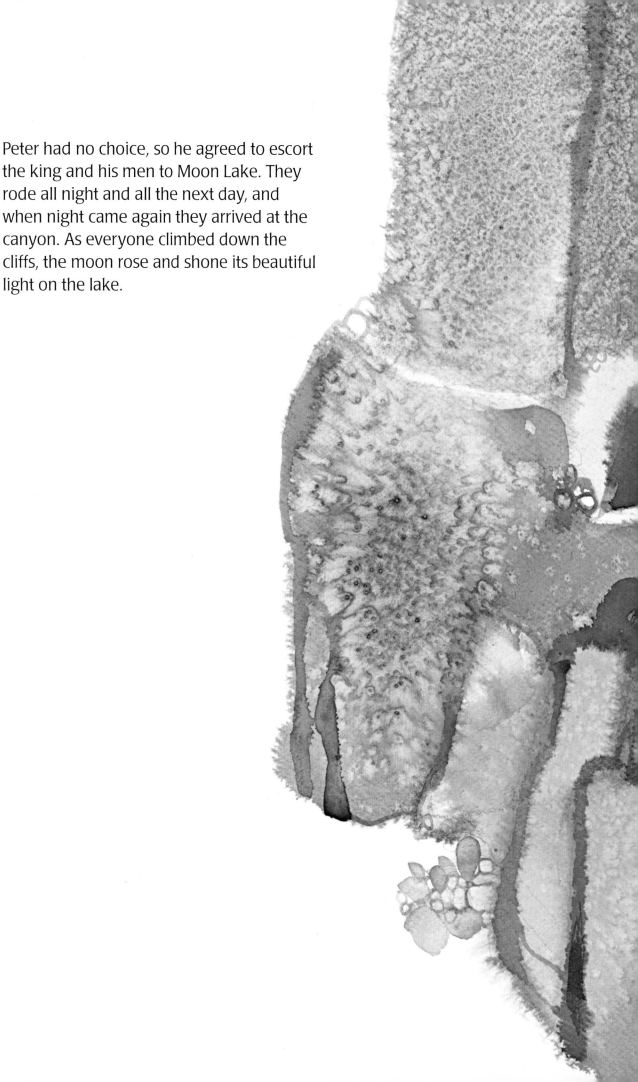

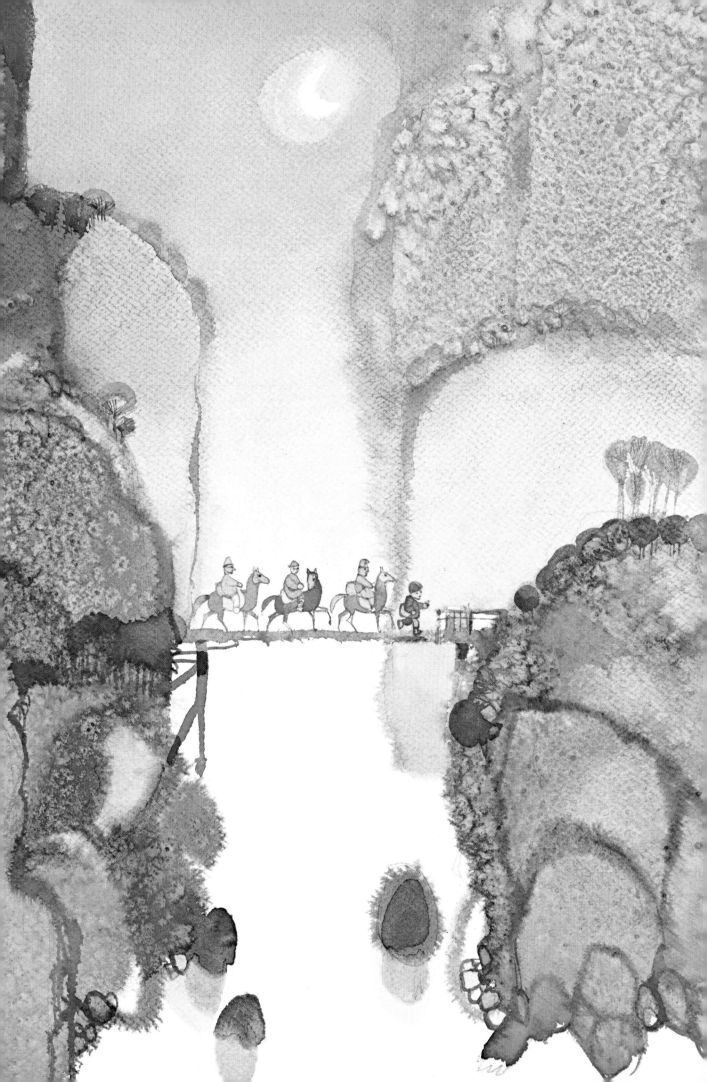

The king and his men quickly started gathering the shimmering stones. Peter himself took nothing. He stared in disbelief as the men greedily stuffed stones into their bags. Then he remembered the words of the fox. "Your Majesty," he said, "we must leave this place before sunrise. Otherwise we will be blinded by the sun."
But the king answered angrily, "Go away! How dare you tell the king what to do!"
So Peter slipped off without saying another word, leaving the king and his men on the banks of Moon Lake.

When the sun rose, the men were instantly struck blind by the dazzling stones. Lugging their heavy sacks, they stumbled among the cliffs and one by one fell into the deep canyon, the precious silver stones tumbling down with them.

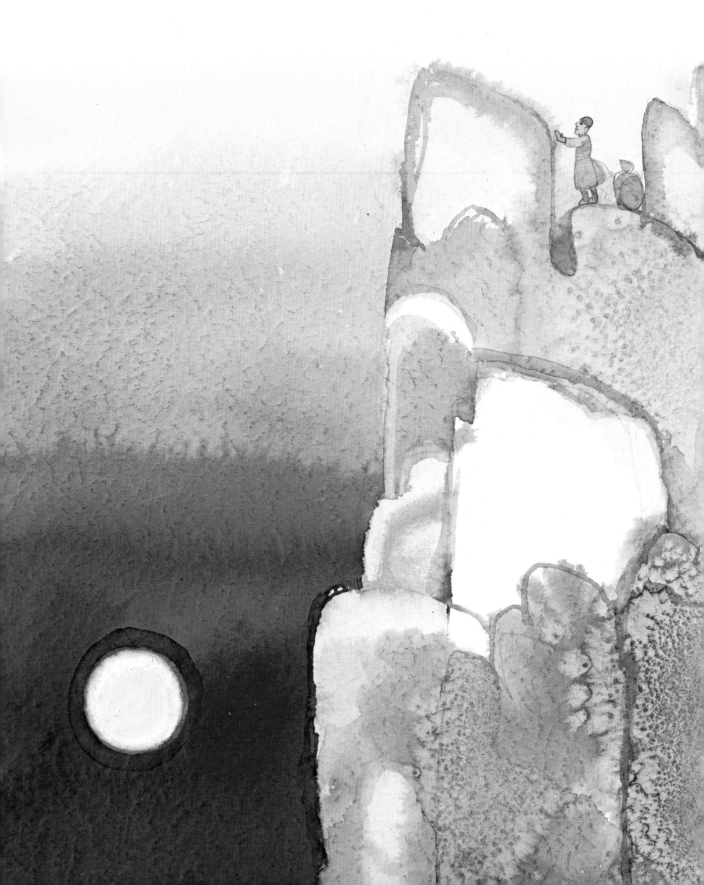

Since no one had seen the king and his men sneaking out of the castle, the people in the town never knew where they had gone. And their lost treasure once again lay gleaming on the banks of Moon Lake.

Peter returned to the lake only once, to collect a few of the stones.
He brought the stones home and tied one to the collar of each sheep.
From then on, no sheep ever got lost, for even at night Peter could
always find them by the glow from the stones.
Peter put the rest of the stones on his windowsill. Whenever there
was a full moon, the stones gleamed so brightly that he could work
long into the night. And whenever his friend the fox came to visit,
he could find his way to the cottage by following the light from
the beautiful silver stones.

Ivan Gantschev studied at the Academy of Art in Sofia, Bulgaria.
Since 1967 he has lived in Germany, working for many years as an
artist at an international advertising agency. He now works exclusively
making picture books for children, among them *The Train to Grandma's*
and *The Christmas Teddy Bear*. His work has been exhibited on four
continents, and his books have been published in sixteen languages.
*The Art of Ivan Gantschev,* a retrospective catalog of his work, is
available from North-South Books.

*Moon Lake* was first published in 1981 by Picture Book Studio. This edition, published
in 1996 in the United States, Canada, Great Britain, Australia, and New Zealand by
North-South Books, has foil stamping and two new images by Ivan Gantschev.

Library of Congress Cataloging in Publication Data is available.

ISBN 1-55858-598-2 (trade binding) 10 9 8 7 6 5 4 3 2
ISBN 1-55858-599-0 (library binding) 10 9 8 7 6 5 4 3 2 1
Printed in Belgium

Other North-South books by Ivan Gantschev
*The Christmas Teddy Bear*
*The Art of Ivan Gantschev*

For more information about this or other North-South books,
visit our site on the World Wide Web: http://www.northsouth.com